Bushels of thanks
to my friends and fellow Shoreline children's book
authors and illustrators; to Bina, Em, Kate D., Kate F., Kay, Lynn, Nancy and Pat;
and to Margery and Brett for helping this book develop from bud to fruit.

With love, N.E.W.

Apples,
Apples,
Apples

Special thanks to Lucille Carr

Library of Congress Cataloging-in-Publication Data

Wallace, Nancy Elizabeth.
Apples, Apples, Apples / written and illustrated by Nancy Elizabeth Wallace.—1st ed.
p. cm.
Summary: Members of the Rabbit family visit an apple orchard, where they have fun picking apples and discovering their many uses. Includes a recipe for applesauce, directions for a craft activity, and sayings about apples.
ISBN 1-890817-19-8
[1. Apples—Fiction. 2. Orchards—Fiction. 3. Rabbits—Fiction.] I. Title.

PZ7.W15875 Ap 2000
[E]—dc21 99-461966

ISBN: 1-890817-19-8
Creative Designer: Bretton Clark
Editor: Margery Cuyler

Written and Illustrated by

Nancy Elizabeth Wallace

WINSLOW PRESS

One blue sky day in early autumn, Dad asked,
"Who wants to go apple picking?"
"Me, me!" yelled Minna.
"Me," shouted Pip.
"Me too," said Mom.

"Let's go!"

They walked down the road to Long Hill Orchard.
"Glad to see you," said Mr. Miller.
"Here are some bags to put your apples in.
What kind do you want to pick?"

"I want apples for pie," said Dad.
"I need apples for crafts," said Mom.
"Yum!" yelled Pip. "I'm going
to pick apples for my snack at school."
Minna whispered, "I want apples for a surprise."

LONG HILL ORCHARD

VARIETIES

Name	Eating	Cooking	Baking	Sweet	Tart	Soft	Crisp
Red Delicious	●			●			●
Golden Delicious	●	●	●	●		●	
McIntosh	●	●	●		●	●	
Granny Smith	●	●	●		●		
Rome Beauty	●	●	●		●		●

"Come look at this chart," said Mr. Miller. "It shows the kinds of apples we grow in our orchard."

"I can't wait to see the apple trees," said Minna.
"Climb aboard!" said Mr. Miller.
They all climbed onto the farm wagon.
Mr. Miller started up the tractor.

"Hold on," he said.

"It's a BUMPY, BUMPY ride."

The sky was blue.
The air smelled crisp and clean. It was a great day for picking apples.

When they got to the orchard, there were apples everywhere! Pip tugged on an apple. The limb shook, and lots of apples fell to the ground. "Uh-oh."

"Try lifting and twisting the apple," said Minna.
"Then pull on it gently. I read that in my apple book."
"Look Minna," said Pip. "Lift, twist, pluck! I can do it.
Lift, twist, pluck."

They all picked

and picked

and picked.

Mr. Miller used a special tool for picking the apples that were hard to reach.

He let Minna and Pip have a turn.

Then Mr. Miller picked up an apple from the ground. He cut it in half.
"It looks like a star inside," said Pip.
Minna said, "I think it looks like a flower."
"It looks like both a star and a flower," said Mr. Miller.

"In fact, apples are a member of a flower family, the rose family."
They counted the seeds.
"There may be as many as ten seeds inside an apple," said Mr. Miller.
"How many seeds do you see?"
"Five!" said Minna.

Mr. Miller cut another apple in half, a different way.
"Look at all the parts an apple has," he said. "You can see the

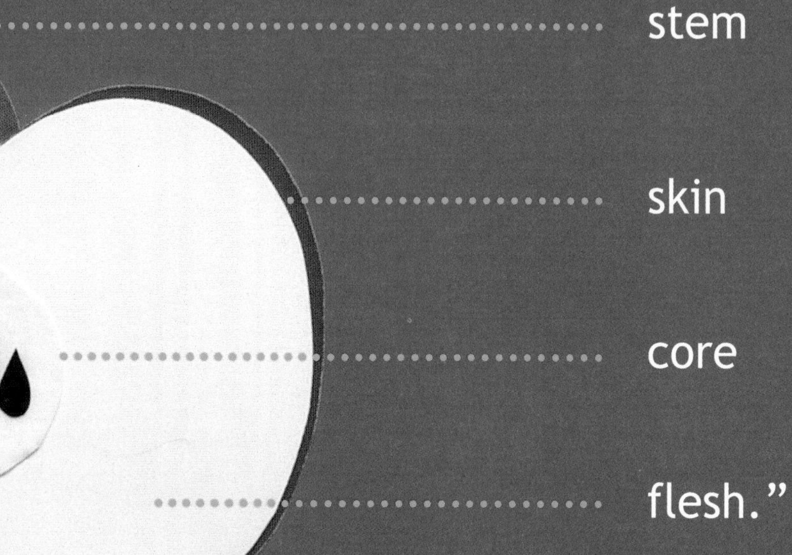

"Did you know that seeds are also called pips?" asked Mr. Miller.
Minna pointed at Pip.
They both giggled.

"Mr. Miller, do you grow trees from seeds?" Minna asked.
"Well, apple trees can be grown from seeds."

He took pictures from his pocket to show them.

"Or, they can be grown the way we grow them at Long Hill Orchard. We graft a branch with buds onto a rootstock." He showed them more pictures.

Minna and Pip looked at the
shiny seeds.
"I'll be Johnny Appleseed,"
said Minna.

"I read about him.
He planted lots and lots
and lots of seeds across
America."

"They grew into apple orchards everywhere."

"Look Minna, I'm Johnny Applepip."

When their bags were filled to the top,
they rode back down the hill.
"Hold on," said Mom.

"whoaaa!"

Minna laughed.
"Hold on to your apples!"

Mr. Miller weighed the bags of fruit
so that he would know how much to charge.
"Apple picking is fun!" said Minna.
"So is apple eating," said Dad.

apple cider
apple cider
apple cider
apple butter
apple jelly
apple jelly
apple butter
apple jelly

When they got home, they had an apple snack. The apples tasted sweet and juicy. Minna looked through her book.
"Here it is!" she said.
"Here's the surprise recipe I want us to try."

"Time to make Minna's surprise recipe," said Dad. Pip washed the apples.
Minna and Mom used a special tool to peel them. Dad sliced and diced them.

1. Wash 6 apples.

2. Peel the apples.

3. Ask an adult to slice or dice the peeled apples.
Put the apples in a pot.

4. Add 2 tablespoons of maple syrup.

5. Add 1/4 cup of apple cider.

6. Ask an adult to bring it to a boil. Shake in cinnamon.
Reduce heat to a simmer, stir, and cook until soft.
It should cook about 20 minutes.

Ask a grown-up to help.

They put the apples, the maple syrup, the cider, and the cinnamon into a big blue pot. Then Mom put it on top of the stove to simmer.

It smelled delicious.

When it was ready, Minna spooned it into bowls.
"Who wants some?" she asked.
"Me, me," said Pip.
"Me," said Mom.
"Me too," said Dad.
They all said, "Yum! Applesauce!"

Minna read

more,

more,

more about apples.

She learned how to make apple prints.

APPLE PRINTING

1. Ask a grownup to cut out the core of an apple for you.

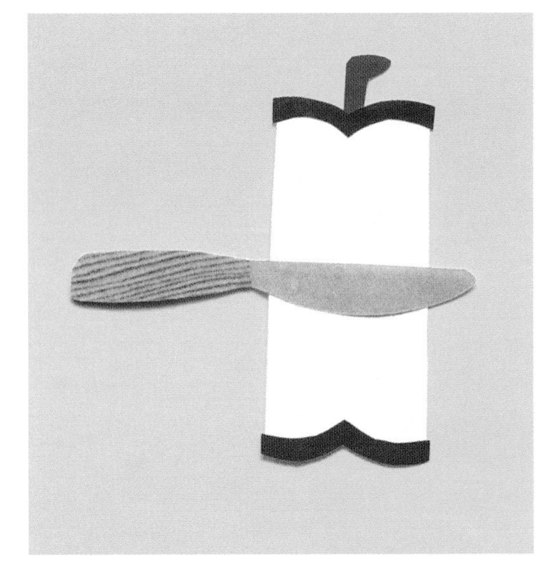

2. (The cut-away part of the apple can be used later for cooking or eating.) Ask a grown-up to cut the core in half.

3. Pick out the seeds from the core.

4. Pour a little paint or food coloring into a plastic lid or aluminum pie plate.

5. Press the apple into the color, making sure that the flesh is coated.

6. Print by pressing the painted apple gently and steadily onto paper.

7. Create the design you like. You can print wrapping paper, writing paper and envelopes, gift cards, bookmarks and more. You can print on paper bags, file cards, and colored and white paper, too.

Minna read about apple sayings

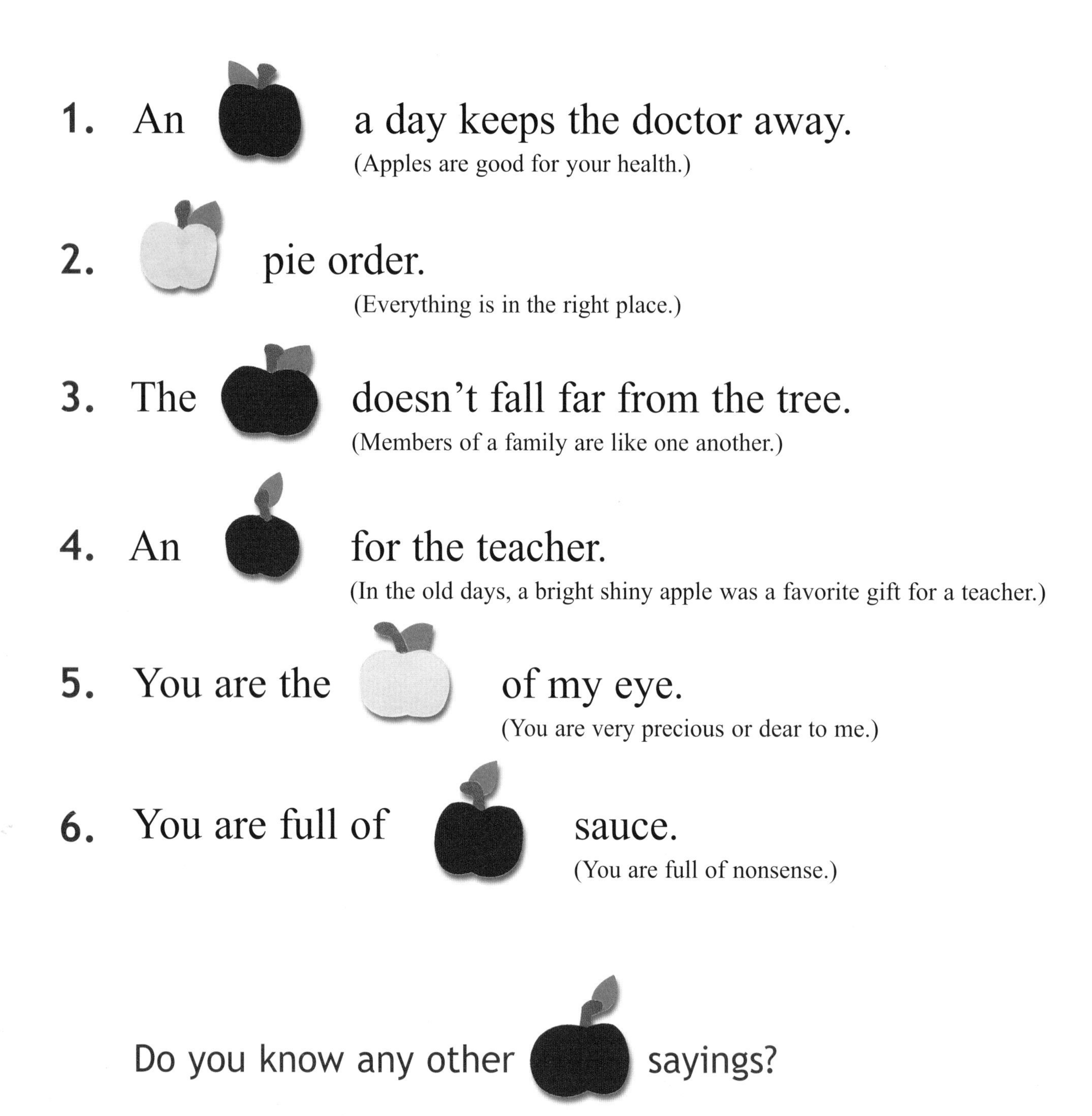

1. An [apple] a day keeps the doctor away.
   (Apples are good for your health.)

2. [apple] pie order.
   (Everything is in the right place.)

3. The [apple] doesn't fall far from the tree.
   (Members of a family are like one another.)

4. An [apple] for the teacher.
   (In the old days, a bright shiny apple was a favorite gift for a teacher.)

5. You are the [apple] of my eye.
   (You are very precious or dear to me.)

6. You are full of [apple] sauce.
   (You are full of nonsense.)

Do you know any other [apple] sayings?

Minna also learned a new apple song from the apple book.

Apple Song

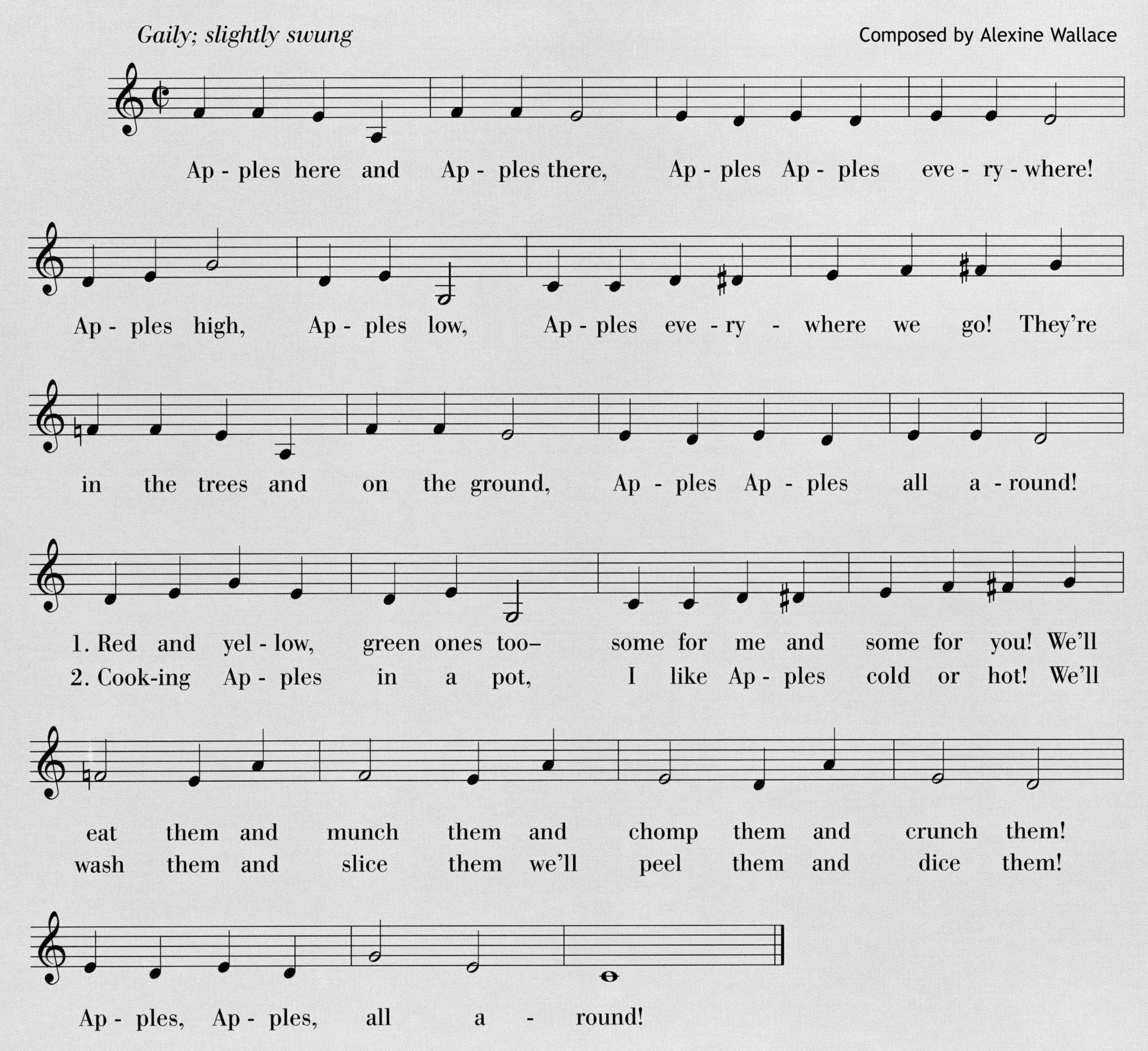

Music engraved by Rowan Sheehan